The Bossy Cockerel

by Margaret Nash

Illustrated by

FRANKLIN WATTS
LONDON • SYDNEY

This edition 2009

Franklin Watts
338 Euston Road
London
NW1 3BH

Franklin Watts Australia
Level 17/207 Kent Street
Sydney
NSW 2000

A CIP catalogue record for this book is available from the British Library.

ISBN 978 0 7496 9141 7

Series Editor: Louise John
Series Advisor: Dr Barrie Wade
Series Designer: Jason Anscomb

Printed in China

Franklin Watts is a divison of
Hachette Children's Books,
an Hachette UK company.
www.hachette.co.uk

Charlie the Cockerel was handsome, but he was also very bossy!

"Cock-a-doodle-doo!"

"Get me this, get me that,"
he said to the hens.

The hens were getting fed up.

Charlie was far too big for his boots.

The hens left one by one.

They began scratching in a new patch of ground.

Suddenly, Hattie the Hen
flapped her wings.

“There’s something buried over here!” she said.

"What is it?" clucked the other hens.

Charlie flew over to have a look.

The hens scratched wildly.
Dust flew everywhere ...

... high up in the air,
and straight into
Charlie's face!

"Stop!" spluttered Charlie.
"It's only a rusty, old bird!"

"Silly, ugly, metal thing."

The hens were very disappointed.

They had their dust baths
and went to bed.

The next morning, they all got a surprise.

The farmer had put the
metal bird on the roof.
It was gold and shiny.

Charlie flew onto the roof.

"Go away!" he cried.

But the bird didn't speak.

Suddenly, the bird turned in the wind.

It knocked Charlie
right off the roof!

The hens laughed until their feathers shook.

"Charlie won't be able to boss *him* around," chuckled Hattie the Hen.

And she was right!

Puzzle 1

Put these pictures in the correct order.
Now tell the story in your own words.
How short can you make the story?

Puzzle 2

bossy rude
kind

surprised angry
lucky

Choose the words which best describe each character. Can you think of any more? Pretend to be one of the characters!

Answers

Puzzle 1

The correct order is:

1c, 2e, 3f, 4a, 5d, 6b

Puzzle 2

Charlie: bossy, rude

Hattie: lucky, surprised